HIGHLAND ELEMENTARY SCHOOL
LIBRARY
Riverside, Iowa 85003

HENRY BABYSITS

To librarians, parents, and teachers:

Henry Babysits is a Parents Magazine READ ALOUD Original — one title in a series of colorfully illustrated and fun-to-read stories that young readers will be sure to come back to time and time again.

Now, in this special school and library edition of *Henry Babysits,* adults have an even greater opportunity to increase children's responsiveness to reading and learning — and to have fun every step of the way.

When you finish this story, check the special section at the back of the book. There you will find games, projects, things to talk about, and other educational activities designed to make reading enjoyable by giving children and adults a chance to play together, work together, and talk over the story they have just read.

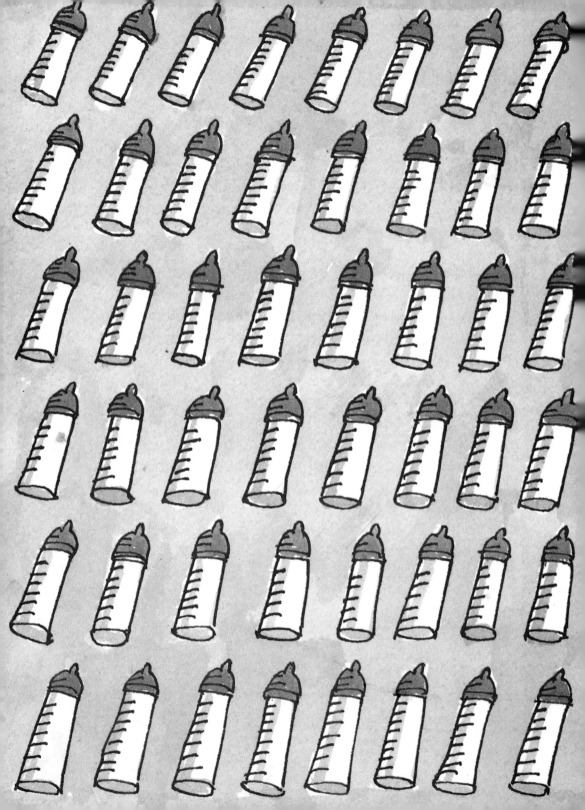

Parents Magazine READ ALOUD Originals:

Golly Gump Swallowed a Fly
The Housekeeper's Dog
Who Put the Pepper in the Pot?
Those Terrible Toy-Breakers
The Ghost in Dobbs Diner
The Biggest Shadow in the Zoo
The Old Man and the Afternoon Cat
Septimus Bean and His Amazing Machine
Sherlock Chick's First Case
A Garden for Miss Mouse
Witches Four
Bread and Honey
Pigs in the House
Milk and Cookies
But No Elephants
No Carrots for Harry!
Snow Lion
Henry's Awful Mistake

The Fox with Cold Feet
Get Well, Clown-Arounds!
Pets I Wouldn't Pick
Sherlock Chick and the Giant
   Egg Mystery
Cats! Cats! Cats!
Henry's Important Date
Elephant Goes to School
Rabbit's New Rug
Sand Cake
Socks for Supper
The Clown-Arounds Go On Vacation
The Little Witch Sisters
The Very Bumpy Bus Ride
Henry Babysits
There's No Place Like Home
Up Goes Mr. Downs

Library of Congress Cataloging-in-Publication Data

Quackenbush, Robert M.
   Henry babysits / by Robert Quackenbush. — North American library ed.
      p. cm. — (Parents magazine read aloud originals)
      Summary: Henry the Duck has his hands full when all the neighbors bring their babies for him to watch one day.
   ISBN 0-8368-0968-8
   [1. Babysitters—Fiction. 2. Ducks—Fiction.] I. Title. II. Series.
PZ7.Q16Hb 1993]
[E]—dc20   93-15472

This North American library edition published in 1993 by Gareth Stevens Publishing, 1555 North RiverCenter Drive, Suite 201, Milwaukee, Wisconsin 53212, USA, under an arrangement with Parents Magazine Press, New York.

Printed in the United States of America

1 2 3 4 5 6 7 8 9 98 97 96 95 94 93

HENRY BABYSITS

by Robert Quackenbush

PARENTS MAGAZINE PRESS · NEW YORK
GARETH STEVENS PUBLISHING · MILWAUKEE

Henry the Duck was enjoying
a quiet day at home
when the doorbell rang.

It was Henry's friend, Clara,
with her baby nephew.
"Would you mind babysitting
for my nephew?" she asked.
Henry was not sure
he knew how to babysit.
"It's easy," said Clara.
"It's my nephew's nap time
and he'll be fast asleep."

Henry said he would be
glad to babysit.
When Clara left, he put
her baby nephew on the couch
and went back
to reading his paper.
The doorbell rang again.

It was Henry's
next-door neighbor.
"I saw Clara bring
her nephew over,"
she said.
"Can you watch my baby, too?
She'll be no trouble."
Henry was a good neighbor,
so he said yes.

As soon as the neighbor left,
the kitten began to cry.
Henry was afraid she would
wake Clara's nephew.
He ran to get some milk
for the kitten.
But he had no milk.
Just then the doorbell rang.

"I heard you were babysitting
this afternoon, Henry,"
said another neighbor.
"Would you please sit
with Baby Amanda?"
Henry saw the bottle of milk
in Baby Amanda's hands,
so he agreed to watch her.

Henry set Baby Amanda down.
He took her bottle and poured
a little of the milk
into a dish.
He gave the milk to the kitten
and the bottle back to Amanda.
Now both babies were happy.
And Clara's nephew
was fast asleep.

Suddenly Baby Amanda
began to cry.
Henry tried burping her,
but that didn't work.
"Maybe she needs changing,"
he thought.
"But I have no diapers."
The doorbell rang again.
It was another neighbor
with another baby.

"I heard you were babysitting,"
said the neighbor.
"Would you please
watch my baby?
He'll be no trouble at all.
He may just need a clean diaper.
When Henry saw
the box of diapers,
he said he would babysit.

In a flash,
Henry changed Baby Amanda
and the monkey, too.
He mopped his brow with relief.
Clara's nephew was
still fast asleep.

Meanwhile the kitten had finished
her milk and wanted to play.
But Henry had no toys.
The kitten started to meow.
Baby Amanda started to cry.
Henry wished he had some toys.

Once again the doorbell rang.
It was still another neighbor
with another baby for Henry.
"Just give him this ball
to play with and he'll be
no trouble," said the neighbor.
Henry took the puppy
and the ball inside.

Quickly Henry tossed the ball
to the kitten and Baby Amanda.
They stopped crying
and started to play.
But the puppy
wanted to play, too.
So he began to chase the kitten.

Round and round the room
ran the kitten and the puppy.
Baby Amanda thought
this was fun.
She began shaking her bottle,
splashing milk everywhere.

The monkey saw Baby Amanda
shaking her bottle.
He thought it would be fun
to throw things.
Lamps and books and flowerpots
went crashing to the floor.

Windows smashed!
Curtains fell!
Henry could not stop
what was happening.

At last it was quiet.
The babies were tired and
they fell fast asleep.
Henry looked around.
Poor Henry.
His house was a mess.

The babies were still sleeping
when the neighbors came
to take them home.
The neighbors thanked Henry
for being such a
good babysitter.

Then Clara came
to pick up her nephew.
She wondered to herself why
Henry's house was such a mess.
But when she saw her nephew
was still asleep she knew
everything was all right.
"You see, Henry," said Clara...

"babysitting is easy."

Notes to Grown-ups

Major Themes

Here is a quick guide to the significant themes and concepts at work in *Henry Babysits*:

- Being willing to help, as Henry is in taking the job of looking after his friend's nephew.
- Making the most of a situation, which Henry does when each new client arrives.
- Sheer fun: your children will love this story, and don't be surprised if you find yourself enjoying this amusing romp, too.

Step-by-step Ideas for Reading and Talking

Here are some ideas for further give-and-take between grown-ups and children. The following topics encourage creative discussion of *Henry Babysits* and invite the kind of open-ended response that is consistent with many contemporary approaches to reading, including Whole Language:

- Let the first reading be just for fun. This book is a beautiful demonstration of what there is to enjoy in reading and why people like to snuggle down with a good book.
- How difficult is it to be a babysitter? If Henry wanted to babysit regularly, what should he have ready in his house? How would he like the babies to behave?
- Was Henry too willing? Should he have said "No?" Are there times when we would like to help someone but it would really be better, safer perhaps, if we refused?
- When Clara came for her nephew, "he was still asleep." This suggests he hadn't awoken and fallen asleep again. Look through the pictures: can your child spot Clara's nephew sleeping in every one?

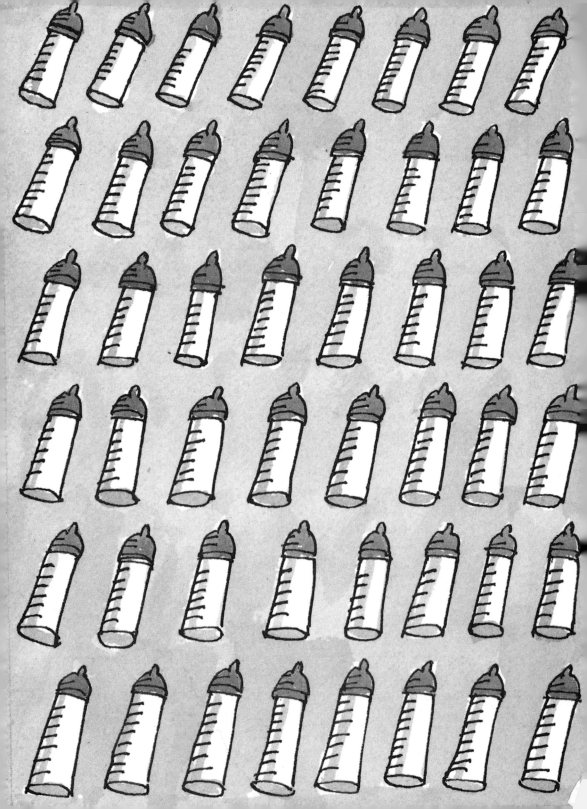

Games for Learning

Games and activities can stimulate young readers and listeners alike to find out more about words, numbers, and ideas. Here are more ideas for turning learning into fun:

You Wear My Hat, I'll Wear Yours

Sometimes putting on the other person's hat can be an educational experience. Role reversing with your child can give you a chance to mirror how your child is behaving in a certain situation and allow your child to see how that behavior feels to the adult taking care of her or him. This is fun to do with positive behaviors (let your child tuck *you* into bed for a nap or make sure you eat all your peas) and very instructional for negative behaviors. If your child has been uncooperative about something, pick a later time that day to play *You Wear My Hat, I'll Wear Yours*. Replay the scene from your child's position and try to use the words and actions your child used, with care not to overdo it. Let the child play the role of powerful parent. Stop the action when you've got a sense of how your child was feeling and when you think your child may have an idea of what it feels like to be the adult in that situation. Then sit down and talk about how it felt to you to be the little person in that situation. Encourage your child to talk about how it felt to be in the adult's position. You may want to discuss what each one of you might have done differently and make a plan to do things differently in the future. Or you may just give each other a hug and let the situation go. Sometimes it is enough just to know how the other person feels.

About the Author/Artist

ROBERT QUACKENBUSH is the creator of the popular Henry the Duck series, which includes *Henry's Awful Mistake*, *Henry's Important Date*, *Henry Babysits*, and *Henry Goes West*. Mr. Quackenbush has also written and illustrated many other books for children.